I AM READING

Tooth Fairy in Trouble

JULIA JARMAN

Il

MIRL

KINGFISHER

KINGFISHER

First published 2008 by Kingfisher
an imprint of Macmillan Children's Books
a division of Macmillan Publishers Limited
20 New Wharf Road, London N1 9RR
Basingstoke and Oxford
www.panmacmillan.com

Associated companies throughout the world

ISBN 978 0 7534 1624 2
Text copyright © Julia Jarman 2008
Illustrations copyright © Miriam Latimer 2008

1 3 5 7 9 8 6 4 2
1TR/1207/WKT/SC(SC)/IISMA/C

A CIP catalogue record for this book is available from the British Library.

Printed in China

Contents

Chapter One

Tooth Fairy was in trouble.

It was getting light, but she hadn't

finished her collecting round on

The Surface.

She had to get back to Fairyland soon.

"Oh no!" she said to herself as she flew
into the next bedroom on her round.
The large boy in bed was waking up.

Tooth Fairy froze. The boy felt under
his pillow – and found his teeth. Two
of them, yucky and yellowy brown.

"MUM!" The boy bawled for his
mother and threw the teeth
on the floor.
"Tooth Fairy hasn't BEEN!"

Tooth Fairy flew
down, found one
tooth, and put it in
her sack.

Then his mother appeared.

"See! No dosh!" said the large boy as
he pointed at his bed.

"But, Norman, your teeth have gone,"
said his mother.

"Look on the floor, stupid!"
said Norman.

Tooth Fairy wanted to fix this horrid
boy with a spell.

But she could feel herself becoming visible.

Her magic powers were draining away.

That is what happens when fairies stay
on The Surface too long.

She dived under the bed.

"What was that?" Nasty Norman
moved surprisingly quickly.

Has he seen me? thought Tooth Fairy,
as he peered under the bed.

Tooth Fairy kept as far back as
she could.

She could see his gappy mouth and piercing eyes. Tooth Fairy was sure the boy could see her. There was a nasty smile on his face.

Suddenly his hand shot forward.

But Tooth Fairy was faster.

Whoosh!

She shot past his hand . . .

. . . up to the window
and out of it.

Chapter Two

"Phew!" said Tooth Fairy, but she saw

the street was busy.

Could she reach the portal to

Fairyland without being seen?

The portal was a little door at the foot
of an old oak tree in Woodland Park.

Whoosh!

"Made it!" said Tooth Fairy.

But a huge dog was lifting its hind leg.

"Open door!
Zaraband!
Whizz me back
To Fairyland!"
She waved her
wand frantically . . .

The dog moved
and the door
opened!
Whizz!
She helter-
skeltered to
Fairyland.

"How lovely to be back!" said Tooth
Fairy, feeling very relieved.

Some Flower Fairies were there.

"Foxglove! Bluebell! Primrose!

I've had a terrible night."

But Bluebell shouted, "Stay there,

Tooth Fairy! We don't want any more

stinky teeth."

"They're not stinky," she said.

Most of them were white and shiny.

"That one is." Bluebell pointed at

Nasty Norman's yucky brown tooth. It

was peeping out of Tooth Fairy's sack.

"There are too many teeth in
Fairyland," said Primrose, more kindly.
"Look at the Tooth Tip.
It's so big. What if it collapsed and
squashed us?"

"Tooth Tip? That's the Royal Tooth Collection," said Tooth Fairy. But she had to admit that it did look dangerous.

"I'll think about it," she replied.
"But what can I do? I'm the Tooth
Fairy," she said to herself.

Collecting teeth and putting money
under children's pillows was her job.
If she didn't do it they would be sad.

The journey to her house was

miserable.

She heard other fairies sing a horrid song,

"Fly away as fast as you can.

Tooth Fairy smells

Like a dustbin man!"

When they saw her coming they flew

away. It made Tooth Fairy sad.

And as if that wasn't enough for poor
Tooth Fairy, back on The Surface
Nasty Norman was setting a trap for
her. He was sticking a tooth to the
floor with glue and he had got hold of
a butterfly net.

Chapter Three

When she got home, Tooth Fairy went straight to bed.

But she was woken up by a Royal Goblin ringing a bell.

"The Fairy Queen wants to see you, NOW!"

"Why?" yawned Tooth Fairy.

"She'll tell you herself," he said.

The Fairy Queen looked very cross.

"Tooth Fairy, I have had lots of complaints.

You are forgetting to collect teeth.

You are forgetting to leave coins.
Last night you missed out a
whole street.
What have you got to say for yourself?"

Tooth Fairy took a deep breath.

"It's so *hard,* your majesty.

There's not enough time.

Surface children go to bed so late, and some of them are horrible, and . . ."

The Queen was tapping her wand impatiently.

"Tooth Fairy, you must start earlier.

You *are* invisible on The Surface."

But not if I stay there too long,

Tooth Fairy thought.

But she didn't say that.

She didn't dare.

Chapter Four

That night Tooth Fairy set off early. But when she reached the portal to The Surface, the Flower Fairies were waiting for her. Dandelion said, "DON'T bring any teeth back, right?"

Tooth Fairy said boldly, "The Fairy

Queen says I must. So there."

But she felt very worried, mostly about

the Tooth Tip.

It did look dangerous.

At first all went well.

In a few minutes her sack was full –
with lovely clean teeth.

Most of the children were great.

They cleaned their teeth.

They didn't eat too many sweets.

One boy had written her a thank you

letter!

Dear Tooth Fairy

Thank you for
leaving me
£1 last
time. x
Love from Joe

It was Joe and his sister, Sylvie, who gave her a very good idea.

They had built a whole village out of building bricks — houses, paths, patios, furniture.

What if fairies built things from teeth?

Tooth Fairy thought.

We could have a Royal Tooth

Recycling Plant!

Longing to get back and tell everyone

her good idea, Tooth Fairy did her

round very fast . . .

. . . until she came to Nasty Norman's.
She'd left him till last.

Chapter Five

At first Tooth Fairy hovered outside.

His tooth was still on the floor.

Should I leave it there? she wondered.

No. The Fairy Queen would be cross.

Whoosh!

She flew in.

Thwack!

A net trapped her.

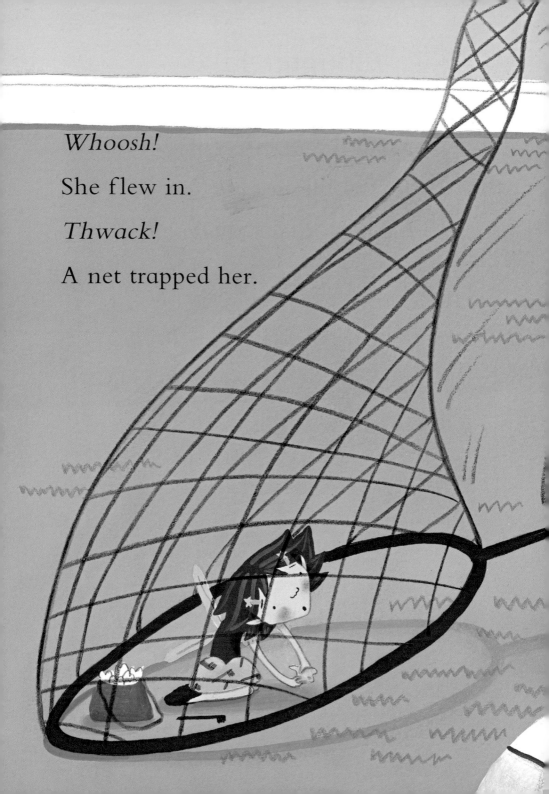

Norman was staring at her.

"Gotcha, Tooth Fairy!"

Tooth Fairy was in big trouble.

She could feel herself becoming visible.

Her fairy powers were draining away.

Hoping she still had some left, she

whirled her wand.

"Izzy wizzy

If you don't let me out!

You'll see your nose

Turn into a snout."

The stupid boy laughed –

and didn't see his nose start to flatten!

"Izzy wizzy

Let me out of here!

Or see yourself

With floppy pig's ears."

He didn't see his ears

start to change.

"Izzy wizzy

Let me out of this jail!

Or see your bottom

Get a curly tail!"

The stupid boy

didn't see his

bottom growing

big and fat.

He didn't see a

curly tail peep out

of his pyjamas.

But his mum did!
"Darling, what's
the matter?"
"Oink!"
Norman's mother
screamed. Norman
dropped the net
and Tooth Fairy
made her escape!

She was soon back in Fairyland.
The fairies thought her Royal Tooth
Recycling Plant was terrific!
Building was fun and they
made lots of useful things.

They made a swimming pool with
stepping-stones, a summer-
house and a new palace
for the Fairy Queen.

"Thank you, Tooth Fairy. You're great!" said the Queen.

"It's a pleasure," replied Tooth Fairy with a big smile on her face.

About the Author and Illustrator

Julia Jarman used to be a teacher and she still spends a lot of time in schools talking to children. She loves writing stories and has published over a hundred books for children. Julia says, "I think some fairies are soppy, but Tooth Fairy is great. She's kind and helpful and brave and I wanted to write a story about her."

Miriam Latimer loves illustrating children's books and has had many picture books published. She always carries her sketchbook with her, and she loves daydreaming and thinking up new characters to draw. Miriam says, "I love the idea of thinking up new ways to recycle, just like Tooth Fairy."

Tips for Beginner Readers

1. Think about the cover and the title of the book. What do you think it will be about? While you are reading, think about what might happen next and why.

2. As you read, ask yourself if what you're reading makes sense. If it doesn't, try rereading or look at the pictures for clues.

3. If there is a word that you do not know, look carefully at the letters, sounds and word parts that you do know. Blend the sounds to read the word. Is this a word you know? Does it make sense in the sentence?

4. Think about the characters, where the story takes place, and the problems the characters in the story faced. What are the important ideas in the beginning, middle and end of the story?

5. Ask yourself questions like:
    Did you like the story?
    Why or why not?
    How did the author make it fun to read?
    How well did you understand it?

Maybe you can understand the story better if you read it again!